WELCOME TO
PASSPORT TO READING
A beginning reader's ticket to a brand-new world!

Every book in this program is designed to build read-along and read-alone skills, level by level, through engaging and enriching stories. As the reader turns each page, he or she will become more confident with new vocabulary, sight words, and comprehension.

These PASSPORT TO READING levels will help you choose the perfect book for every reader.

READING TOGETHER
Read short words in simple sentence structures together to begin a reader's journey.

READING OUT LOUD
Encourage developing readers to sound out words in more complex stories with simple vocabulary.

READING INDEPENDENTLY
Newly independent readers gain confidence reading more complex sentences with higher word counts.

READY TO READ MORE
Readers prepare for chapter books with fewer illustrations and longer paragraphs.

This book features sight words from the educator-supported Dolch Sight Words List. This encourages the reader to recognize commonly used vocabulary words, increasing reading speed and fluency.

For more information, please visit passporttoreadingbooks.com.

Enjoy the journey!

Cover design by Carolyn Bull.

Little, Brown and Company
Hachette Book Group
1290 Avenue of the Americas, New York, NY 10104
Visit us at LBYR.com

First Edition: September 2017

Little, Brown and Company is a division of Hachette Book Group, Inc. The Little, Brown name and logo are trademarks of Hachette Book Group, Inc.

The publisher is not responsible for websites (or their content) that are not owned by the publisher.

Library of Congress Control Number 2017940899

ISBNs: 978-0-316-47203-6 (pbk.), 978-0-316-47201-2 (ebook), 978-0-316-47205-0 (ebook), 978-0-316-47202-9 (ebook)

Printed in the United States of America

CW

10 9 8 7 6 5 4 3 2 1

Passport to Reading titles are leveled by independent reviewers applying the standards developed by Irene Fountas and Gay Su Pinnell in *Matching Books to Readers: Using Leveled Books in Guided Reading*, Heinemann, 1999.

Licensed By:

Photo credits: page 3 race car © Kuznetsov Alexey / Shutterstock.com; page 6 and 7 photo of racetrack © EPG_EuroPhotoGraphics / Shutterstock.com; page 8 photo of Formula One race car © Natursports / Shutterstock.com; page 8 photo of stock car © Action Sports Photography / Shutterstock.com; page 9 photo of dragster © Christopher Halloran / Shutterstock.com; page 9 photo of off-road truck © Rodrigo Garrido / Shutterstock.com; page 9 photo of kart racer © Neil Lockhart; page 10 and 11 photo of racetrack © Oskar SCHULER / Shutterstock.com; page 12 photo of car engine © Lena Pan; page 13 photo of a pit crew © Photo Works / Shutterstock.com; page 14 photo of the Monaco Grand Prix © NAN728 / Shutterstock.com; page 14 photo of the Daytona 500 © Action Sports Photography / Shutterstock.com; page 15 photo of the Dakar © Christian Vinces / Shutterstock.com; page 16 and 17 photo of monster truck © Silvia B. Jakiello / Shutterstock.com; page 18 photo of Brutus monster truck © Christopher Halloran / Shutterstock.com; page 18 photo of Gravedigger monster truck © Natursports / Shutterstock.com; page 19 photo of Bigfoot monster truck © Maksim Shmeljov / Shutterstock.com; page 19 photo of Swamp Thing monster truck © Pavel L Photo and Video / Shutterstock.com; page 20 photo of trucks racing © Barry Salmons / Shutterstock.com; page 20 photo of truck doing donuts © Paul Stringer / Shutterstock.com; page 21 photo of truck doing backflip © Dave Kotinsky / Stringer; page 21 photo of truck doing a wheelie © Barry Salmons / Shutterstock.com; page 21 photo of truck running over a car © bogdanhoda / Shutterstock.com; page 22 photo of tires © Vladimir Melnik; page 23 photo of corn © Jiang Hongyan; page 23 photo of truck © Pavel L Photo and Video / Shutterstock.com; page 23 photo of killer whale © Tory Kallman; page 24 photo of monster truck landing © Felix Mizioznikov / Shutterstock.com; page 25 photo of monster truck (right) © Felix Mizioznikov / Shutterstock.com; page 26 photo of crash © Action Sports Photography / Shutterstock.com; page 27 photo of emergency workers © Rattanapon Ninlapoom / Shutterstock.com; page 28 photo of police officer © sirtravelalot; page 28 photo of paramedic © Tyler Olson; page 29 photo of firefighters © SanchaiRat.

TRAINING ACADEMY

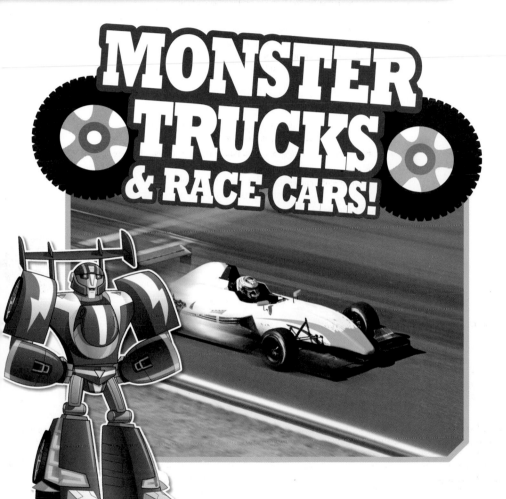

MONSTER TRUCKS & RACE CARS!

By Trey King

LITTLE, BROWN AND COMPANY
New York   Boston

Cody is writing manuals for
the Training Academy.
Blurr says, "We should
do a book about race cars."

"And monster trucks, too," adds Cody.

"Great idea," says Optimus.

"I know where to start...."

Auto racing is a sport where drivers race cars for fun and prizes.

Almost as soon as cars were invented, people began to have races.

Who wants to race me?

FUN FACT

The first car ever invented was not powered by gas but by steam!

There are many kinds of races. **Formula One racing** takes place all around the world. **Stock-car racing** is very popular in America.

Formula One

stock car

dragster

off-road truck

kart racer

In **drag racing**, cars drive in a straight line to see which is fastest.

In **off-road racing**, vehicles drive through deserts, rocky areas, and other rough places.

Kart racing is for people of all ages. The cars are much smaller.

FUN FACT

One of the fastest cars is the Hennessey Venom GT. It once hit 270 miles per hour.

FUN FACT

A Formula One car's exhaust gets so hot that it can melt aluminum!

Check out all these amazing facts I found!

Cars and other vehicles can move
because of their **engines**.
An engine uses energy, like electricity
or burning gasoline, to move the vehicle.

In a race, the **pit crew**
has one job: fix a car
as fast as possible.

FUN FACT

It takes a pit crew less
than three seconds to
replace the tires on a
car during a race.

The **Monaco Grand Prix** takes place in the streets of Monte Carlo.
The **Daytona 500** in North America has a large cash prize.
Cars drive around a track 200 times.
It takes place in Florida.

The Dakar is an off-road event.
Cars go through sand dunes, grass,
rocks, and more!

A **monster truck** begins
as a normal truck or car.
But it has much larger
tires added to it.

Monster trucks used to be side acts at racing events. Now they have their own shows called **rallies**.

FUN FACT

Most monster trucks are at least *12 feet tall*. That's twice as tall as a human adult!

Monster trucks usually have themes or styles.

Some are painted like animals, dinosaurs, or monsters.

Others are inspired by movies or games.

Brutus

Gravedigger

Bigfoot

Swamp Thing

At a monster truck rally, the vehicles do lots of wild things. Here are just a few:

race each other,

drive in circles (called donuts),

20

do backflips,

drive with the front wheels in the air (called popping wheelies),

and run over and crush other cars!

21

I think I need bigger tires!

All monster trucks have one thing in common: giant tires! They also have hard skeletons to keep the drivers safe.

FUN FACT

Many monster trucks have supercharged engines that run on methanol, a corn-based oil.

ENERGY of FREEDOM
MONSTER MANIA SHOW

FUN FACT

The world's longest monster truck measures 32 feet long. That's the same size as an orca whale!

Monster truck rallies started
in the United States.
They have since become popular
in other places.

There has been an accident!

Sometimes accidents
happen at sporting events.
But people on staff are
ready to help.

Police keep people calm and away from the accident.

Emergency workers are ready to help if anyone is hurt.

Firefighters put out the fire.

Whew! Good thing they were prepared!

The Rescue Bots are always ready to help.

29

"I have learned a lot today," Cody says.

"Can I drive a monster truck now?"

"Not until you are older," says Optimus.

The other Rescue Bots have a good laugh.

Hello, Rescue Team cadets!
Go back and read this story again—
but this time, see if you can find these words!

dragster

engine

tires

corn